GW00858453

The Higgledy-Piggledy PIGEON

By Don M. Winn
Illustrated by Dave Allred

OTHER CARDBOARD BOX ADVENTURES BOOKS BY DON WINN

Chipper the Clown

Chipper and the Unicycle

The Tortoise and the Hairpiece

The Incredible Martin O'Shea

Shelby the Cat

Superhero

The Watch Cat

Twitch the Squirrel and the Forbidden Bridge

Available in hardcover, softcover and eBook formats

Take the stories to the next level with interactive versions from InteractBooks.

www.interactbooks.com

The Higgledy-Piggledy Pigeon Special Hardcover Edition
ISBN: 978-1-937615-09-3
Copyright © 2010 by Don M. Winn

Published by Cardboard Box Adventures
www.donwinn.com

Printed in the United States. All rights reserved under International Copyright Law. Cover and/or contents may not be reproduced in any manner without the express written consent of the author.

*This book is dedicated to the many educators that go the extra mile
to help and encourage those with learning challenges to succeed!*

HOW TO USE THIS BOOK:

Cardboard Box Adventures books are books worth talking about. They are designed to give parents and children an opportunity to have meaningful discussions about important topics. The stories are just the beginning. Please read them aloud together and then use the questions included at the end of the stories to begin conversations with your children. Many of the questions will help you to see how well your child understood the story. Others will help you and your children talk about what's on their minds and what's important to them. The last section of questions is designed to help kids become active thinkers, inspiring their creativity and imaginations.

INTRODUCTION:

Does the fact that Kryptonite is a weakness for Superman make him any less super? No one would ever say that! The truth is that all people have some kind of challenge that makes life a little harder. But it doesn't mean they can't do things!

Sometimes our personal challenge can make it hard to do ordinary things. Sometimes other people can tell that we have a hard time with something. That can make us feel upset or embarrassed. But no matter how hard a challenge may seem, we can still succeed with determination and the right kind of help. Albert Einstein couldn't read until he was nine, but look what he accomplished once he did!

This story is about a young homing pigeon named Hank who finds out on his first day of flight school that he has a learning difficulty. Hank's learning challenge has to do with a special talent that (almost) all homing pigeons have.

Let's see what happens as Hank comes face to face with his Kryptonite...

A young pigeon named Hank,
a beginner in rank,
began his first day of flight school.
Like his father before,
he was ready to soar,
and in his flight cap he looked cool!

"We have taught the best,"
the teacher professed,
"Now it's time to see what you can do.
Like Sir Isaac Pigeon
and Leonardo da Pigeon,
there's potential in each one of you."

They checked understanding
of takeoff and landing,
and the students were measured and scored.
Each test was a breeze
so Hank finished with ease,
and was perched for the Pidgie Award.

Hank was feeling delight
'bout his first solo flight
as each student was given a task.
He must deliver a note
that his teacher wrote,
and then find his way back to the class.

With goggles and cap,
his assignment and map,
Hank quickly took off on his flight.
Though the class headed east,
he went off to the west,
'cause he couldn't tell left from right.

With his map upside-down,
Hank looked all around,
and was puzzled on which way to fly.
He would go to the left
when he should have gone right,
and was just about ready to cry!

When nothing looked right
at each leg of his flight,
Hank figured he must be off-course.
He did not want to ask,
but to finish his task,
he stopped to get help from a horse.

"Pardon me, Horse,
but I can't find my course.
Can you tell me please where I should go?"
"Since day after day
in this pasture I stay,
I'm sorry to say I don't know."

Then he asked a large snail
who was oozing a trail,
"Can you tell me please, what trail to make?"
"I take many days
just to go a short ways,
so your guidance I can't undertake."

A raccoon overheard
and chimed-in with a word,
"For your cap, I can show you the route."
Already delayed,
he agreed to the trade,
and was shown a straightforward way out.

With a worn tattered map
and missing his cap,
he arrived almost two hours late.
The class snickered and stared
because he had erred...
he was ready to quit from heartbreak!

The teacher took him aside
and told him with pride,
"Don't be sad because some things are hard.
Though you had a rough start,
you have talent and heart,"
and proceeded to read his score card.

"Your takeoff and landing
are truly outstanding,
for which you've received a high score.
And your altimeter reading
and speed of proceeding
will shorten delivery chores."

"But your sense of direction
could use some correction,
and though you have failed on this score,
with hard work on your side
and a compass to guide,
to the head of the class you can soar!"

With a compass to use
there was no time to lose,
so Hank practiced the rest of the day.
By final inspections,
he'd learned his directions,
and completed the class with an "A"!

QUESTIONS PARENTS CAN DISCUSS WITH THEIR CHILDREN

1. What problem did Hank have?

2. How did Hank feel when he got back to class and his classmates were laughing at him?

3. Why did he feel better after his teacher talked to him?

4. How did Hank respond to the teacher's suggestions about using a compass to find his way?

5. Have you ever felt sad or mad when something wasn't easy for you?

6. Does having a personal hardship or learning challenge mean that you can't succeed?

7. Do you know anyone who uses a special tool (like Hank's compass) to overcome a personal hardship or learning challenge?

8. When something is hard for us, why is it better to keep trying rather than to give up?

QUESTIONS FOR ACTIVE THINKING

1. What do you imagine is Hank's favorite color? His favorite place to play? His favorite book? His favorite food? What kind of sports do you imagine he is good at? What is his house like?

2. Where do you imagine Hank will travel now that he can use a compass? What kinds of places do you think he would like to visit? Where would you like to travel?

3. What makes a good teacher? If you were a teacher, how would you help your students?

4. A compass has a needle that always points north. How would this be helpful to Hank? If you were lost in the woods, would you like to have a compass with you? Why? What else would you like to have with you?

5. If you have trouble learning some things, what could you do to make it easier? Are there any tools you can use to help you learn?

6. Has your teacher ever helped you? How? Did that make you happy? What could you do or say to let your teacher know that you are happy he or she helped you?

ABOUT THE AUTHOR

Don Winn has been writing since 1998. He started by writing poetry and then moved on to writing rhyming children's picture books. He is surprised that he likes to write so much because he remembers that when he was in school, he would do anything he could to avoid writing. Don Winn lives in Round Rock, Texas, with his wife and two cats.

Don Winn is the author of the Cardboard Box Adventures series of children's picture books, which includes the titles *The Tortoise and the Hairpiece*, *The Higgledy-Piggledy Pigeon*, *Superhero*, *Chipper the Clown*, *Chipper and the Unicycle*, *The Incredible Martin O'Shea*, *Twitch the Squirrel and the Forbidden Bridge*, *The Watch Cat*, and *Shelby the Cat*.

Visit his website at www.donwinn.com for more information and all the latest news.

ABOUT CARDBOARD BOX ADVENTURES

Don Winn calls his series of books Cardboard Box Adventures because he remembers how much fun he had as a child using his imagination while playing with a simple cardboard box. The box could be anything he wanted it to be: a spaceship, a cave, a fort, a submarine...the possibilities were endless!

Some of his other favorite memories involve the times his grandmother would read aloud to him and talk about what they had read together. He is grateful to her for doing this because he knows now that it always reassured him of her love for him and her interest in his thoughts and feelings.

With his books, Don hopes to fuel kids' active imaginations, share some helpful object lessons, and provide opportunities for parents and children to reinforce their loving bond through conversations about important topics.

Lightning Source UK Ltd.
Milton Keynes UK
UKHW050419220222
399035UK00002B/19